FREE TO BE INCREDIBLE ME

Written By

Joelle-Elizabeth Retener

Illustrated By

Connor DeHaan

MW00957507

On his first day of school,
Manny came home feeling blue.

He had learned something he never knew.

He learned that there were things that

"BOYS JUST SHOULDN'T DO."

This made dad **SAD** and quite certainly **MAD!**

Until he thought a great thought...
that wasn't half bad!

He would model all the behavior that boys
"JUST SHOULDN'T DO" to prove to little Manny...

That such things just weren't true.

So they rocked vibrant colors—not

just boring ole **BLUE**.

They **COOKED** and they **BAKED,**

they learned to **SHIMMY** and **SHAKE,**

and they cried and cried during every **HEARTACHE**.

They tried buns, braids and
color but settled on ponytails

TO SHOW OFF THEIR FLAIR.

Manny learned that he didn't
need to fight just to prove his
might and that he could be

a **LOVER**, a **FEELER** and
DELICATE, too!

The more they did together, the
more Manny's **CONFIDENCE** grew.
Manny unlearned all the negative
things that he knew.

Manny realized that people would talk
and judge, no matter what you do.

So in end, the most important thing—

is to just be YOU!

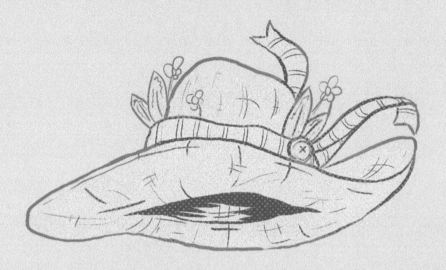

To an amazing husband and father.
Thank you for always seeing the
"Incredible" in all of us.
J-E.R.

No part of this publication may be reproduced in whole or in part, stored in a retrieval system, or transmitted in any form or by any means, electronic, mechanical, photocopying, recording, or otherwise, without prior written permission of the publisher. For information regarding permission, write to the publisher, StoryBook Genius, LLC. at: 219 Jackson Street, Augusta, MO 63332 or visit them at sbgpublishing.com
ISBN 978-1-949522-20-4 Text copyright© 2019 by Joelle-Elizabeth Retener
Illustrations copyright© 2019 by Joelle-Elizabeth Retener
All rights reserved.
Published by StoryBook Genius, LLC.
Printed in the U.S.A.

STORYBOOK
GENIUS PUBLISHING
sbgpublishing.com

yip jar Book
Design by
yipjar.com

CPSIA information can be obtained
at www.ICGtesting.com
Printed in the USA
BVHW020628070519
547542BV00004B/16/P